The Crabtree Chronicles

The Diddle of
the Sphinx

The Crabtree Chronicles

The Diddle of the Sphinx

Hodder
Children's
Books

a division of Hodder Headline plc

Text and illustrations copyright © 1998 Robin Kingsland

Published in Great Britain in 1998
by Hodder Children's Books

A Catalogue record for this book is available from
the British Library

ISBN 0 340 69991 4

Typeset by Avon Dataset Ltd, Bidford-on-Avon, Warks
Printed and bound in Great Britain

Hodder Children's Books
A division of Hodder Headline plc
338 Euston Road
London NW1 3BH

*Thanks to Carol Andrews, in the
Egyptology Department at the British Museum*

This . . .

is Eddie Crabtree

Eddie is an ordinary boy, living in an ordinary town, doing ordinary things. But Eddie has some extraordinary ancestors.

Like his Ancient Egyptian ancestor Ka Rahb T' Re, known to everyone as Scarab.

This is Scarab's story...

1

Scarab lived in Ancient Egypt, although, of course, it wasn't ancient when he lived there. He liked drawing, and playing with his best friend Ra Bhit. But most of all, Scarab liked going to visit his uncle, Hip Horah.

As far as Scarab was concerned, Hip Horah was the best uncle in the Nile Delta. In spite of his important job – he was an architect and a tomb builder for the royal household – he always had time for his young nephew. Scarab and Ra Bhit were in and out of the workshop all the time. Uncle

Hip would sit them down in the corner and
give them reed pens, ink and sheets of
papyrus. Then, while he worked on

drawings or models for his latest building
project, they could draw too. If he was in an
especially good mood, he'd get cool Nile clay

11

from a back room, and they'd make little
figures for fun.

Just lately, though, Scarab's uncle had
not been his usual self.
He was looking tired,
listless, down in the
dumps. In short
he was looking
thoroughly
fed up.

"Pyramids!" said Uncle Hip between gritted teeth. "That's all I ever hear these days. Pyramids! Pyramids! Pyramids! This week was a perfect example. One of Pharaoh's ministers wants a tomb building – he reckons he's only got twenty years to live, so he wants to get his after-life sorted out now. I, though I say it myself, go in with a really classy design – a long avenue of pillars with scenes from their life all around and a papyrus leaf pattern at the top; a really stylish tomb, with paintings on the wall, loads of lapis lazuli, and a lovely, elegant sarcophagus."

15

"Well, it's lovely ... but —"

My wife really has her heart set on one of those PYRAMID thingies

Like the one you did for Mrs. Snefaru.

"Honestly, pyramids! I mean where's the challenge in designing something like that? I just don't see the point."

"It's the bit at the top," said Ra Bhit, helpfully.

A few days later, Scarab and Ra Bhit were in the workshop when there was a commotion outside. The boys went to find out what the fuss was about, and Scarab came back with an excited gleam in his eye – and an idea!

"Well?" asked his uncle. "What was all that about?"

"Pharaoh's just arrived back from a hippo hunt, and apparently he bagged the biggest hippo anyone's ever seen!"

"That's great news," cried Ra Bhit.
"Not if you're the hippo," the builder muttered gloomily.

"Cheer up, Uncle," Scarab said. "There's something else. Pharaoh is so pleased with himself, that he's decided to mark the event with a monument: The Great Hippo-Hunt Monument. He's holding a competition to decide who's going to design it. And you, Uncle Hip, are going to enter!"

You see, one day, when Hip Horah had gone to get some clay from his back room, Scarab had taken a sneaky peep inside. What he had seen had made his jaw drop with admiration. On a low, mud platform in the corner were dozens of little clay models:

19

Pharaohs, High Priests,
officials, gods –

each one a perfect likeness, with intricate details of face and jewellery and costume. Uncle Hip had a secret hobby, and what's more, he was really good at it!

"No more pyramids, Uncle!" Scarab declared. "You're going to enter that competition. You're going to win it. And Pharaoh will make you his sculptor-in-chief!"

"I'm going to enter that competition. I'm going to win it, and Pharaoh will make me his sculptor-in-chief!"

This was not Uncle Hip speaking. A few miles away, in a huge gloomy chamber cluttered with artefacts and furniture, the priest Ihnstep was talking to his pet baboon, Nefer Nefer. The baboon wasn't really that bothered about her master's ambitions. She was more interested in getting at the figs she could see on the table.

But Ihnstep could think of nothing but the competition, for one very good reason . . .

Ihnstep had been a pretty powerful person in the days of the old Pharaoh. He had lived at the royal palace and had a great deal of influence, and his frequent bribe-taking had been overlooked because he was a cousin, twice removed, of the queen. Then the old Pharaoh had died, a new Pharaoh had taken over and cousin Ihnstep was

removed for a third time – this time by
physical force.

Now he lived in a shabby house in a shabby
back street, and all that remained of his old
life were two shabby assistant priests that
he kept around to do his dirty work.

And there was plenty of that to be done,
all with one ultimate goal – to get Ihnstep
back into the royal household. And since the
priest fancied himself as a bit of a sculptor,
the mention of Pharaoh's competition had
got him very excited indeed.

"I didn't know you did statues an' that,
boss!" said Khoppet, the bigger of his two
cronies, and by far the stupidest.

"You, Khoppet, know very little about anything at all!" the priest sneered.

They were looking at Ihnstep's collection of models. "I like this frog!" said the other assistant, a small, weaselly man known as Squuiffi.

"That's not a frog, imbecile, that's a crocodile!" Ihnstep snapped.

"Yeah," said Khoppet, pointing at another model. "*This* is the frog!"

"No, no, no!" Ihnstep shrieked. "That is a bust of my dear, departed second cousin, the late queen!"

He hastily covered his sculptures. "I suppose I can't expect morons like you to appreciate great art." He bustled them out of his dingy work room.

"Well, good luck, boss," said Squuiffi. "You'll need it. They say every sculptor in Egypt is going in for this competition."

"Oh, you leave them to me," the priest said, with a dark smile.

You see, Ihnstep had a secret weapon – Shuttit, the fork-tailed rat-god. Shuttit worship had been banned by the new Pharaoh because of the god's reputation for helping the wicked. But when all his efforts at flattery and crawling had failed to get him back "in" with Pharaoh, Ihnstep had become a secret, but devoted, rat-god follower.

25

So it was, that the moment his two goons had left, Ihnstep went upstairs to a small dark, back room. It wasn't even a room really – more like a tiny cell. The ceiling and walls were blackened by smoke from a single oil-lamp, which now glimmered feebly before the small figure of a god. The statuette had the body of a man, but its head was that of some kind of rodent. It actually looked like a lopsided guinea pig, or possibly a hamster with one cheek full of food, but it was supposed to be a rat. Needless to say, Ihnstep had made it.

"Let me see," he muttered, as he prepared ritual offerings of bread and fruit. "It's three days to the competition." The dark smile spread across his face again. "Time for an epidemic, I think." He bowed before the rat-god's altar. "Hear me, oh great Shuttit . . ." he droned, "and grant your servant's wishes . . ."

2

The next day, news of the Great Hippo-Hunt
Monument contest spread like wildfire. So
too did a mysterious illness. All over the two
kingdoms and across the length and breadth
of the Nile Delta, sculptors were going off
sick. From bad colds to backpain, from gippy
tummy to chronic toothache, they were
dropping like flies.

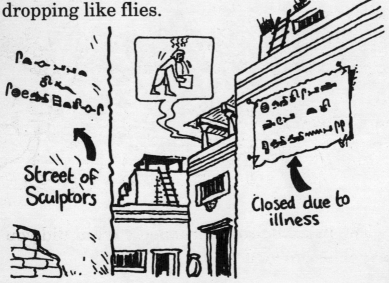

Street of
Sculptors

Closed due to
illness

"It worked, Nefer Nefer!" Ihnstep gloated to his beloved baboon, feeding her yet another fig. "The god has done me proud. Not a sculptor in Egypt is able to work. Mine will be the only entry in the competition!"

"You haven't heard about this Hip Horah then, boss?" Khoppet said, as he and his partner stepped into the priest's chamber.

The priest's brow darkened. "What did you say?" he growled.

"Hip Horah," Khoppet repeated, "the builder. He's entering the competition too. And the word on the street is, his design's pretty snazzy!"

"Yeah," Squuiffi agreed, "I heard that Pharaoh's vizier's seen the drawing, and thinks that Pharaoh will love it!"

Oh please Uncle Hip — just a quick peek!

Scarab had heard this rumour, too, but he still couldn't persuade his uncle to give him a sneak preview of the design.

"Oh, go on, Uncle," the boy had pleaded.

"No."

"But, Uncle. If Pharaoh's vizier has seen it . . ."

"Who told you that?"

"Practically everybody!"

"It's just a silly, idle rumour. Look, I happen to be very superstitious, and I think

30

it would be bad luck for anyone to see my model before Pharaoh himself."

"Oh please, Uncle—"

"No! And that's final!"

But all Hip Horah's secrecy had only made the gossip spread faster. So now the word was well and truly out that the builder had come up with a very special design . . . a real contender.

"Curses!" Ihnstep spat. He paced his room furiously. Why hadn't the magic worked on

Hip Horah? What could have gone wrong? How could Shuttit have left that stupid tomb-builder off the list? Then he stopped. Of course! That's what had happened. He had asked the rat god to make *sculptors* sick, and that's just what Shuttit had done.

Only Hip Horah, like Ihnstep, wasn't officially a sculptor. So he'd escaped. And it was too late now to nobble him. His design was ready, his model finished, waiting to be picked up by the royal assistants first thing in the morning. Ihnstep chewed his nails. He couldn't do anything about it . . .

unless . . .

"Meet me at midnight," he told his two henchmen. "And bring your grave-robbing tools! We're going to pay a little visit to our builder friend."

"That'll be nice, boss," said Khoppet. "I'd like to meet him."

"Idiot," Ihnstep growled. "He won't be there!"

"Then why are we going?"

"To steal his design, of course!"

"How can you be sure he won't be there, Boss?" Squuiffi asked.

"Because Lord Shuttit and I are going to see to it!" the priest replied, with a malevolent smile. "Now go!"

As
soon
as his two
henchmen
had left, Ihnstep
climbed once more
into his secret cell.

"Oh, Lord Shuttit of the sharp teeth," he intoned. "I have another tiny favour to ask . . ."

3

Scarab lay awake. He just couldn't sleep. Tomorrow morning Uncle Hip Horah's drawing and model would be whisked off to the royal palace. And he, Scarab, hadn't even seen it. Ra Bhit was staying at his house for the night. Scarab went and shook his friend till he woke.

"We've got to go to Uncle's," he whispered.

"It's the middle of the night," said Ra Bhit groggily.

"I know, but I just have to see Uncle's design. And the palace officials collect it first thing tomorrow."

Everyone in the house was asleep. They crept out, and made their way through deserted streets.

"This is a wild goose chase," Ra Bhit grumbled. The workshop will be closed."

Scarab shook his head. "Uncle's planning to stay up all night, to guard the drawings and the model. I heard him telling his assistants this afternoon, so I know."

They came to the workshop door. "Yoo hoo!" Scarab called softly, as the two friends stepped into the dimly lit workshop. "It's only us, Uncle."

Suddenly a figure loomed out of the gloom and came straight towards them with a spear raised high. The boys stood frozen in terror.

Then Scarab saw who it was.

"Uncle Hip!" he gasped in relief. "You gave us such a scare!"

Strangely, his uncle didn't answer. He didn't even seem to notice they were there. Staring straight ahead, he walked past them and out into the night.

"Uncle?" Scarab called. "Uncle? I thought you were guarding the shop tonight?" The children ran after the builder as he hurried in the direction of the river. Scarab and Ra Bhit both tugged on his arm.

"Come back!" Scarab wailed. "Where are you going?"

"Fishing," said Hip Horah in a flat, hollow voice.

"Fishing?" Scarab was flabbergasted. "But . . . but you've never been fishing in your life!"

"It's never . . . too late . . . to start!" came the flat voice again.

Surely midnight is a <u>bit</u> late?

But it was useless. No matter how hard the boys tried, they couldn't even slow the builder down. He strode mechanically on, like one of his own statues brought to life.

"There is definitely something weird going on," Ra Bhit murmured.

With a cold rush of panic, Scarab thought about the workshop, and his uncle's design sitting there, unprotected. "Quick!" he cried. "Let's get back!"

They ran all the way. Picking up the lamp that still burned on the table, they peered

around the room. Everything seemed in
order. The drawing was still there,
tied up in its papyrus roll, and
the model stood on a bench,
wrapped in a cloth bag,
ready for collection.

"Looks like we're on guard now!" Ra Bhit
said.

"Oh well," Scarab whispered, "as long as
we're here and Uncle isn't, I don't suppose it
would do any harm to have one little
peep . . ."

He tiptoed over to the bench, leaned
across, and was just untying the cloth bag
when—

"Someone's coming!" Ra Bhit hissed.

Panic! Low voices outside came nearer and nearer. Any second now they would be discovered. Scarab looked frantically round for somewhere to hide.

Moments later, Ihnstep the priest and his two henchmen jostled in.

"Anybody home?" the priest called.

As if I didn't know!

"Shame he left the door open," said Khoppet sadly. "I was looking forward to breaking in."

Ihnstep saw the model standing in its wrapping on the bench. A clay tablet identified it as the contest entry. "Bring that!" he commanded.

"Er . . . Boss?" said Khoppet, as he lifted it. "Won't it be a give-away if you enter this bloke's model? I mean, if the vizier's seen it, well . . ."

"Ah, Khoppet," the priest sighed, "the embalmers will have such an easy time with you when you finally pass to the underworld."

"Ah, thanks, boss," the lunk said, flattered. Then his brow furrowed. "Why's that, then?"

"*Of course* I'm not going to hand in *his* model. I shall copy it – adding a few improving flourishes of my own, naturally – and then I shall utterly destroy this one. As long as Pharaoh likes the design, do you really think the vizier will make trouble? Besides, without a model, Hip Horah will be out of the competition and – Thoth's your uncle – I, will win! Where is his drawing, by the way? We might as well take that too."

Khoppet and Squuiffi shrugged. They hadn't seen it.

"It must be here!" said the priest. "Keep looking! There's a reward for whichever one of you . . . WAIT!"

"Why boss?" asked Squuiffi. "Are you going to say ready, steady, go?"

But it wasn't that. Ihnstep had noticed Nefer Nefer, the baboon, pawing at something by the door. It was a mummy case. Hip Horah kept it there to show potential clients the high quality of work they could expect from his firm. Ihnstep signalled to his two cronies, and they glided silently to the wall. Then, at a signal from their boss, they grabbed the case and threw it open!

45

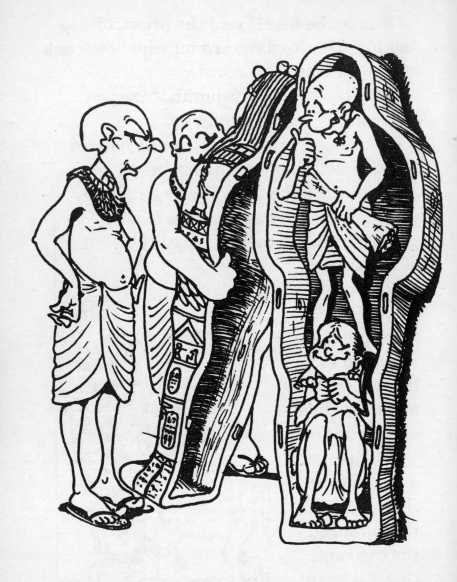

"Er . . . Good evening," Scarab said nervously. "Room for one more on top?"

"They must have heard everything!" snarled the priest. "Bring them too."

4

Scarab and Ra Bhit were frog-marched through a dark warren of mud-brick houses until they reached Ihnstep's seedy dwelling.

"Don't worry!" said Ihnstep, as the two boys looked anxiously around his cluttered chamber. "I won't detain you long. Just until after the judging." Taking the stolen model from Khoppet, he carried it, still in its bag, through to an ante-room. Scarab watched him go.

Through the door, he could see a small table with a fresh lump of clay sitting on it, waiting for the priest to copy Uncle Hip's design.

The two boys were sandwiched between Khoppet and Squuiffi, well away from the door. Khoppet had a tight hold of Nefer Nefer's lead, and the irritating animal was dividing its time between nipping Ra Bhit's leg and straining to get away.

"The two big baboons I can cope with," Ra Bhit whispered, "but the little one's really getting on my wick!"

Scarab looked down at the grinning, scampering, chattering animal.

And had an idea.

Very slowly, very carefully, Scarab leaned over, as if he were about to scratch his leg.

Instead, he reached for the baboon's collar.
He felt around till his fingers closed on a
little metal clasp. Then he squeezed.

No sooner had she heard the
"click", than Nefer Nefer was
off. She shot through the
door like a scalded cat,
and was halfway up the
alley before Squuiffi
or Khoppet
knew what was
happening.

"Er . . . boss."
Khoppet called.
"Fools!" the priest
squealed, when they told
him what had happened. "That is a
sacred animal!" and he ran out of the
building calling Nefer Nefer's name.

The two henchmen looked at each other, hesitating. "Tsk, tsk, tsk," said Scarab, shaking his head and giving them a look of enormous sympathy. "Lost the boss's prize monkey, have we? He's going to be so-o-o cross if he can't find her!"

Khoppet gulped and looked at Squuiffi.

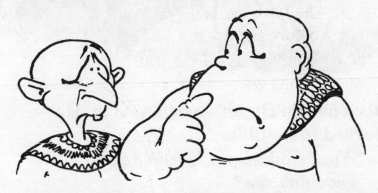

Then they both said, "Stay there or else!" and scrambled out of the door to help their master in his search.

"Quick Ra Bhit!" Scarab hissed. "We don't have much time."

They ran into the ante-room. "Let's just get Uncle's model and . . . Oh, no!" With horror Scarab saw that the walls were lined with dozens of cloth bags – all identical to

the one Hip Horah's model was in. He
turned to Ra Bhit.

"Where did he put Uncle's model?"

"I couldn't see."

"Oh great. That's just great!"

"Well I can't see through walls. Can you?"

"All right, all right. Let's not argue."
Scarab started running round, pulling the
bags from model after model. Each one was
more awful than the last.

"Huh!" Scarab said bitterly, looking at a
clay chair – or a clay cat, he couldn't be sure
which. "Uncle would have *walked* it. He still

could, if only we could find his model." He looked round. Ra Bhit was hunched over a roll of papyrus on the table. "Don't dither about," cried Scarab. "Keep looking!"

Ra Bhit left what he was doing and rejoined the search. The two boys tore frantically round the room, opening every sack they could lay their hands on.

"Oh this is hopeless," Scarab groaned. "Old Pebble-Head must have hidden it somewhere!"

"Is *this* what you're looking for?" said a voice behind them. The boys turned slowly.

Khoppet and Squuiffi leaned against the wall, wheezing and out of breath. Nefer Nefer sat on the floor, showing her teeth and making a noise that sounded suspiciously like a snigger.

But Scarab wasn't looking at any of them. He was looking at Ihnstep, and the cloth sack that swung from the priest's outstretched fist.

Scarab made a quick mental calculation. If Ra Bhit could create a diversion, and if he, Scarab, moved fast enough, he could grab the bag and be out of there before Ihnstep and his stooges knew what had hit them.

A tiny flame of hope began to flicker in him.

It was still flickering as the priest let go of the bag.

Everything seemed to slow down. Scarab watched in open-mouthed horror as his uncle's work fell. He heard the muffled smash of breaking clay as the sack

hit the ground.

Ihnstep smiled a slow, wide and entirely unpleasant smile.

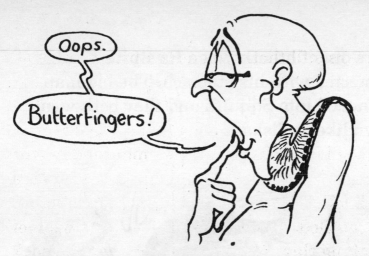

"RUN, RA BHIT, RUN!" Scarab yelled. He snatched up the bag, grabbed the papyrus roll from the table, put his head down and charged for the doorway.

Ihnstep's cronies were still out of breath from monkey chasing. Khoppet was even more out of breath when Ra Bhit's head connected with his stomach. The big man cannoned into Squuiffi and they both went down like obelisks.

Scarab almost made it to the door. But then he felt a scrawny hand grasp his long side-lock. He winced as his head snapped back. Another hand snatched the papyrus. "I'll take that!" said the priest. Scarab fought to get it back, but Ra Bhit was dragging him out of the door, and away up the dark street.

"Let me go!" Scarab protested, close to tears. "he's got the drawing!"

"Never mind that!" his friend said. "Just RUN!"

Khoppet ran after the boys. "We'll get 'em, boss!" he growled, but Ihnstep called him back.

"They cannot harm us now," he said, patting the papyrus roll lovingly. "I have all I need."

He went to the table and carefully cut the reed band that held the scroll together. With a sigh of joy and triumph he spread the drawing before him. Khoppet and Squuiffi peeped over his shoulder, eyes alive with drooling excitement. But the drool dried up quite quickly when they saw what was drawn there.

"Er . . . boss," Khoppet murmered.

"I know, I know!" the priest snapped. "It's a little . . . unusual. But if Pharaoh's vizier has approved it, who are we to argue? Now leave me. I have a lot of work to do before sunrise."

As soon as they realised that they weren't being followed, Scarab and Ra Bhit stopped running and collapsed under some trees. Then they made their way back to the workshop.

It was exactly as they'd left it. Hip Horah still hadn't returned. Stumbling over to the table in the dark, Scarab opened the bag. There was a crash of cascading crockery.

"Careful!" Ra Bhit whispered. "You've knocked over some of his other models!"

"Oh, no!" Scarab cried, when Ra Bhit

brought the lamp. "We'll never sort this lot out!

The officials will be here in a couple of hours, and all we've got is a pile of rubble – Ihnstep has the drawing! He's won!"

"No he hasn't," Ra Bhit turned to his friend with a huge grin on his face.

"What are you talking about?" Scarab said. "He took the drawing out of my hand!"

"No," Ra Bhit said. "He took *a* drawing. He didn't take *the* drawing. You see, when those two goons dragged us out of here, I managed to, well . . . pick up a papyrus. Another papyrus. I hid it in my kilt, and back there, while you were looking for the model, I did a swap!"

"Why Ra – you're a Bhit of a genius!"

"So you see, the real drawing is . . ." Ra-Bhit reached behind him, "is . . ." His face fell as he realised it had gone. "I had it tucked in my kilt when we left the priest's place, honest. It must have fallen out while we were running."

"Well, we can't go back now," Scarab said. We'll just have to do what we can with this."

The two boys turned and looked down at the little pile of pottery shards on the floor.

"How hard can it be?" said Scarab, with a shrug.

"Sure," said his friend, without much conviction. "I'll, er . . . get some wet clay, shall I?"

When Hip Horah returned the next morning, he was astonished on three counts.

Firstly, he had woken up on the banks of the Nile, disturbed by a bunch of women nearby trying to pull a basket out of the reeds nearby.

Secondly, he was in possession of a basket full of fish that he could not account for.

And thirdly, when he finally got back home, he found his nephew and friend slumped over the workshop table, caked with clay and fast asleep.

"Hello you two," he said.

Scarab and Ra Bhit woke groggily, rubbing red eyes and yawning.

"How was your fishing trip?" Scarab asked, as soon as his mouth could work.

"What fishing trip?" Hip Horah asked. Scarab and Ra Bhit explained about his strange exit the night before. They carefully avoided mentioning Ihnstep's visit, or its awful consequences.

"Well, well, how extraordinary," said Hip Horah. "I don't remember any of that. One minute I was sitting where you are now. Next thing I knew, I was waking up with my face in a basket of fish."

"Mmmm, Ni-i-ice!" said Ra Bhit, feeling slightly queasy all of a sudden.

"Anyway, I'm back here in one piece. That's the main thing."

That phrase "in one piece" made Scarab's blood run cold. He wanted the underworld to open up and swallow him.

"By the way," his uncle went on, "was the model picked up all right?"

"Er . . . well," Scarab answered, "it *was* picked up, but . . ."

"Great. I'll tell you what. I'll wash and change and then, if you like, you can come to the judging with me."

Scarab swallowed hard. He'd been on at his uncle from the start to let them watch the judging. Now that they were actually being invited, he could suddenly think of things he'd rather do.

Like be boiled in oil, for instance.

6

A big crowd had gathered for the judging.
Everyone had turned out, knowing that the
young Pharaoh was coming in person to
choose the winning model. His beautiful
queen would be there too. Everyone was
jostling excitedly, eager to catch a glimpse of
the royal couple.

Right at the front of the crowd, Scarab
could see a canopy. Under it, half a dozen
models sat wrapped in their linen bags
waiting for the great unveiling. A few
sculptors must have dragged themselves
from their sick-beds to get late entries in.

A warm wind gusted across the courtyard,
carrying on it the sound of cymbals and
trumpets, lutes and tambourines. Pharaoh
had arrived. At least the front end of his
procession had.

Forgetting everything in their excitement, Scarab and Ra Bhit pushed forward – and found themselves just a few feet from Ihnstep and his henchmen. The old priest grinned like a Nile crocodile. As far as he was concerned, the prize commission was . . . well . . . in the bag.

The two boys watched in wonder as the procession came down the wide avenue towards them. First the dancing girls, leaping and swaying to the music. Then the girls of the royal orchestra. Behind them a troop of royal guards with spears pointing skyward. After them, a dozen priests, and

then, finally, the Royals themselves,
gleaming in snow-white robes and dazzling
multi-coloured collars. Slaves behind
them wafted cooling palm fans.

The people cheered
and kept on cheering as
Pharaoh and his wife made
their way to a double throne under
a second canopy. The "fan club" took up
their positions behind the throne. Pharaoh's
vizier mounted the podium, and the crowd
fell silent.

"Great Pharaoh . . ." began the vizier. "Thou art the Centre of the Centre of the Four-pillared World. Thou art the Sun God Ra stepping down from the Heavens. Thou art . . ."

"Yes, yes, yes," said the King, wriggling impatiently in his seat, "I know what I art! Let's skip all that and get to the good bit. Unveil the entries."

The vizier looked hurt, but he knew better than to argue with a Pharaoh.

"Very well, Your Majesty." He turned to

the crowd. "And now . . . the moment you've all been waiting for: the final entries for the great Hippo-Hunt Monument."

"There aren't very many, are there!" the queen said, looking bored. "I put my best wig on for this. I hope I haven't got all dressed up for nothing!"

The vizier muttered something about a shortlist. Then, with as much showmanship as he could muster, he began to remove the cloth bags.

Scarab watched impatiently as, one by one, the models were revealed. There were little smatterings of applause, and cheers from each artist's friends and family, but the models were fairly "ho hum", and Mr and Mrs Pharaoh didn't look too excited.

Only two bags left now. Uncle Hip Horah's and Ihnstep's. Which would come out of its bag first? The vizier took hold of a cloth, and pulled.

The crowd gasped. Some of them even laughed. Ihnstep, who had looked nervous for a moment, now giggled openly. The vizier had unveiled Hip Horah's model.

Or rather, what was left of it. From the back of the crowd, Scarab could hear his uncle's wail of horror.

The two boys had done their best, but there had been so little time. It had been late, they'd both been exhausted, and they hadn't had much practice at gluing broken models together. With the best will in the world, it was a bodge job. Great lumps of clay held the thing in one piece. Not only that, but there were bits of three models all jumbled up together. Pharaoh's head was there, sandwiched between a crocodile and an ibis head – except that Pharaoh's face had the ibis's beak and the ibis wore Pharaoh's crown. Pharaoh's hands were sticking out from under the croc, which seemed to have sprouted wings, and the whole jumbled pile was sitting on the hippo's head.

The vizier quickly covered the model, and glared across the crowd at Hip Horah, who had gone as white as his kilt.

"I missed it!" Pharaoh complained.

"There's been . . . a mistake, Oh Lord of the Two Niles!" the vizier gibbered, and without a pause he stepped to the next bag. Pharaoh leaned forward – he wasn't going to miss this next entry.

"This is the entry of the priest Ihnstep, Oh Son of the Sun."

"Oh, him," Pharaoh groaned. "Oh well, let's see it anyway!"

The vizier took a hold of the cloth . . .

"Not that it matters any more," Scarab whispered miserably to his friend, "but which drawing *did* you leave there last night?"

Ra Bhit grinned from ear to ear. "One of yours," he said.

one of MINE?!

Scarab's mouth dropped open. He looked

up, appalled, just in time to see the cover whipped from Ihnstep's model.

It was well made. No question. Old Ihnstep had excelled himself. The model was the best thing he'd ever done; The Double Crown of Egypt, the cobra symbol at the front, the long thin neck of the young king, they were all perfect. Perfect too were the other details of Scarab's drawing – the cross-eyes, the tongue sticking out, the two thumbs in the ears, and the fingers so well sculpted you could almost see them waggle, almost hear the raspberry sound the statue was trying to make.

If the cobra on the crown had been real, the vizier might have jumped back faster, or screeched louder, but not much. He almost dived under the table to hide from such a monstrously insulting image.

Ihnstep hadn't quite twigged yet. He'd been so sure of winning that he was already crowing to his cronies when the royal guards grabbed him. The priest was frog-marched up to the royal presence. The vizier laid into him.

"How dare you present this . . . this . . . thing!" he screamed.

"I don't understand . . ." Ihnstep gasped. "You said Pharaoh would love it!"

"I? I've never seen it before."

"You have. I was told you'd seen it at Hip Horah's worksh—"

He stopped. He had blundered. Given the game away.

"I have never been to Hip Horah's workshop," the vizier said slowly, "but *you* obviously have."

A ripple of outrage ran through the crowd. The priest had submitted a stolen design. What a scandal!

"Take him away!" Pharaoh commanded.

The vizier shrugged hopelessly. "Well, Oh Bringer of the Life-giving Inundation, that appears to be that. We'll re-advertise next week."

"What a fiasco!" the queen snorted. "Come on dear, let's go hunting!"

"Wait a minute!" Pharaoh said, getting up.

"What about the other one? The one I didn't see."

"Oh, but Your Majesty, it is unworthy—"

"Never mind the clap-trap," Pharaoh commanded. "I want to see it."

"But, Bringer of Harvest, Thresher of the Corn of Life—"

"Well, you'd know all about corn!" the young king snapped, and reaching past the vizier he took the bag off himself.

Uncle Hip Horah was up on the platform in a second, grovelling before the Bringer of Harvest, who was staring silently at the mish-mash image before him.

"Oh, Pharaoh!" he wailed. "I abase myself before you. There has been a terrible mistake. I will destroy this travesty . . . I will grind it underfoot . . . I will eat the dust of it before you . . . I will . . . I will . . ."

"I *love* it!" cried Pharaoh. "I will make a cleaned-up version!" said Hip Horah.

Scarab nearly fainted. Pharaoh liked the model? He must be dreaming. But he wasn't.

"It's rough, obviously," the young king was saying. "But I get the idea. Yes. Yes. Like the Sphinx, only . . . Sphinxier. Me with the strength of the crocodile, but the grace of the ibis, crushing the hippo. It's different. It's fresh. It's . . . it's *now*! Don't you think?"

The vizier nodded so hard his head nearly flew off.

"You took the words out of my mouth, Oh . . . Taker of Words out of My Mouth!" he beamed.

On the way home, Scarab's uncle got a full explanation of what had gone on.

"Well, I *should* be furious with you," he said. "But it wouldn't seem fair, since you won me the commission."

Scarab knew all about the commission. It was chiselled into a hunk of rock, and he was carrying it!

"Royal Sculptor-in-Chief!" Uncle Hip
Horah said, loving the sound of it. "And best
of all . . ." he sighed happily, "no more
pyramids!"

A few weeks later, the queen ran into the vizier in the royal palace.

"What's happened to that little weasel Ihnstep?" she asked sweetly. "I haven't seen him for a while?"

"He's working on the Great Hippo-Hunt Monument, Oh Daughter of the Rain Giving Skies," replied the vizier.

"But I thought this Hip Horah chappie was designing it," said the queen.

"Oh, he is, Oh Wind That Brings Life to the Reed Beds. I only said that Ihnstep was 'working on it'."

Also by Hodder Children's books

THE CRABTREE CHRONICLES

Robin Kingsland

Book 1: LET'S GET CAESAR!

Eddie Crabtree – an ordinary kid with an ordinary life. But Eddie's ancestor's were anything but ordinary. Take young Marcus Crabbius, way back in Roman times . . .

Caesar's birthday looms, and Marcus Crabbius is fed up. The great general, Gaius Agrippa, is coming to stay for the celebrations, along with his daughter – the dreadful Druisilla. What a total bore . . .

But when Marcus and Druisilla find themselves involved in a terrible conspiracy against Caesar, the excitement is rather more than they bargained for.

Oh, for a bit of peace and quiet!

Also by Hodder Children's books

THE CRABTREE CHRONICLES

Robin Kingsland

Book 2: BLAME IT ON THE BARD!

Eddie Crabtree – an ordinary kid with an ordinary life. But Eddie's ancestor's were anything but ordinary. Take young Perkin Crabbetrie, way back in Tudor times . . .

Perkin's passion is the theatre. He longs to see a play performed – maybe one by that Mr Shakespeare. But Perkin's parents don't approve at all!

Perkin, however, is determined. And when he finds himself in the new town playhouse. Perkin cannot believe his luck . . .

But what happens next makes him rather wish he'd stayed at home . . .

Also by Hodder Children's books

THE CRABTREE CHRONICLES

Robin Kingsland

Book 3: FRANKIE AND THE FÜHRER

Eddie Crabtree – an ordinary kid with an ordinary life. But Eddie's ancestor's were anything but ordinary. Take young Frankie Crabtree, back during the Second World War . . .

Frankie and her little brother Sam are evacuees – staying in the heart of the country – with not a lot to do. The pigs are all very nice but . . . well . . . Frankie wouldn't mind a bit of excitement now and again.

But coming face to face with Hitler himself, is not quite what Frankie had in mind!

Can Frankie take on the Führer and win?

THE CRABTREE CHRONICLES

0 340 69989 2 Book 1: Let's Get Caesar!   £3.50 ☐
0 340 69966 3 Book 2: Blame it on the Bard!   £3.50 ☐
0 340 69991 4 Book 4: The Diddle of the Sphinx £3.50 ☐

*All Hodder Children's books are available at your local bookshop,
or can be ordered direct from the publisher. Just tick the titles you
would like and complete the details below. Prices and availability
are subject to change without prior notice.*

Please enclose a cheque or postal order made payable to
Bookpoint Ltd, and send to: Hodder Children's Books, 39
Milton Park, Abingdon, OXON OX14 4TD, UK.
Email Address: orders@bookpoint.co.uk

If you would prefer to pay by credit card, our call centre
team would be delighted to take your order by telephone.
Our direct line *01235 400414* (lines open 9.00 am–6.00 pm
Monday to Saturday, 24 hour message answering service).
Alternatively you can send a fax on *01235 400454*.

TITLE	FIRST NAME	SURNAME

ADDRESS
DAYTIME TEL:	POST CODE

If you would prefer to pay by credit card, please complete:
Please debit my Visa/Access/Diner's Card/American Express (delete
as applicable) card no:

Signature .... Expiry Date: ....

If you would NOT like to receive further information on our products
please tick the box. ☐